The Chester Books of Madrı

1. THE ANIMAL KINGDOM

Edited by Anthony G. Petti

For Damian

CONTENTS

Chester Music

8/9 Frith Street, London, W1V 5TZ
Exclusive distributors: Music Sales Ltd., Newmarket Road,
Bury St. Edmunds, Suffolk, IP33 3YB.

Cover:
May (Taurus/Gemini) from the
Très Riches Heures du Duc de Berry.
Reproduced by kind permission of the Musée Condé, Chantilly.

1. IL BIANCO E DOLCE CIGNO

The gentle white swan sings while dying, and I approach the end of my life weeping. How strange and different a fate, that he dies disconsolate and I die happy in a death that fills me with joy and desire. If I were to feel no other pain in my death I would be happy to die a thousand times. (Alfonso d'Avolos)

Jacob Arcadelt (c. 1505–68)

† ♩ 𝄽 emended from ♩. *Alto and Tenor switched 29-33i.

2. CONTRAPUNTO BESTIALE ALLA MENTE
(The animals improvise counterpoint)

Text: Fa, la, la. Woof-woof, meow, hoo, cuckoo.
Bass: A hunchback is untrustworthy; so is a cripple.
If a braggart be good, put it down in the history books.

Adriano Banchieri (1568 – 1634)

* Canto I & II are switched in bars 13-28.

* Animal noises ad lib., silence, then solitary cuckoo (Ed.)

8

* A solitary bass hiccough is an effective anticlimax. (Ed.)

3. THE SILVER SWAN

Orlando Gibbons (1583 – 1625)

4. EL GRILLO

The cricket is a fine singer who can hold a long note. Sing, cricket, about carousels. The cricket is a fine singer, but he is not like the other birds: as soon as they have sung a little while, they are off on business elsewhere; but the cricket always stays put. When the weather is at its hottest, then he sings solely for love.

Josquin des Près (c. 1440 – 1521)

* two minims in original (halved notation).

*Repeat sign bar 17 and not 22 in the original.

14

5. AUDITE NOVA

Hear the good news! The farmer from Dimchurch has a fat goose, a goo-goo-goose! It has a long, fat, thick, widely-curving neck. Bring this goose here, take it, my dear Hans: pluck it, stuff it, broil it, roast it, carve it, eat it! This is St. Martin's precious bird, to whom we must not be an enemy. Young Heinz, bring us first-rate wine and pour it out boldly: don't dawdle! In God's name let us drink good wine and beer to this boiled goose, this roasted goose, this tender goose, lest it should do us harm.

Orlandus Lassus (1532–94)

18

6. PETITE IMPORTUNE MOUCHE

Bothersome little fly, how lucky you are: while you are buzzing around my beloved gathering a thousand sweet delicacies, I spend every day in bitterness. How happy I would feel to be able to avail myself of the licence you have to touch and sip the whole neck, and to kiss the white breast, the brow, the hair, and that bright eye. You hover over her to place your feet on her head, and within the gold of her hair you take comfort: how happy I would feel to be able to do the same. However, if you go so close to her eyes to amuse yourself, you wretched creature, you will find to your cost there, I fear, that all suddenly bursts into flames, proving that one must not be so bold.

Claude Le Jeune (c. 1530 – 1600)

* To be sung also after verses 1 and 2.

20

* Presumably to be sung either in addition to the 3-part setting or as an alternative to it.

7. DER GUTZGAUCH

The cuckoo sat on the fence; it rained hard and he got wet. Then the sun came out: the cuckoo became sleek and dry. Then he spread his wings and he flew from there across the lake.

Lorenz Lemlin (c. 1496 - 1549)

* Sop. 1 and Sop. 3 are reversed in the original.

8. UNE PUCE

I've a flea in my ear, alas! which night and day itches and bites me and drives me mad. No one can give me
me remedy. I run hither and thither. Remove it from me, take it out, I beg you. O fairest one, help
me. When I think to give my eyes over to sleep, it comes to sting, itch and bite me, and prevent me from sleeping.
I am helped by an old enchantress who cures everyone and everything, but does not know how to cure me.

Claude Le Jeune (c. 1530 – 1600)

1. U - ne pu - ce j'ai de - dans l'o - reille, hé - las!
2. Quand mes yeux je pen - se li - vrer au som - meil,
3. D'u - ne vieil - le char - me - res - se ai - dé me suis,

Qui de nuit et de jour me fré-till' et me mord, et me fait de-ve-nir fou.
El - le vient me pi-quer, me dé-mange, et me point, et me gar - de de dor - mir.
Qui gué-rit tout le monde, et de tout gué-ris-sant, ne m'a su me gué-rir moi.

26

4. Bien je sais que seule peux guérir ce mal, Je te prie de me voir de bon oeil, et vouloir m'amollir ta cruauté.

9. DOLCISSIMO USIGNOLO

A 5 voci, cantato a voce piena, alla francese

Most sweet nightingale, you call to your beloved mate, singing: come, my soul. But song is of no avail to me, and I have no wings to fly as you have. Happy little bird, kind nature rewards you well in your delight, and though she denied you knowledge, she gave you good fortune. (Giovanni Battista Guarini)

Claudio Monteverdi (1567 – 1648)

32

10. IL EST BEL ET BON

"My husband is lovely and good, neighbour." Two women from the same neighbourhood were asking one another: "Have you got a good husband?" "My husband is lovely and good, neighbour. He does not anger me or beat me. He does the housework and feeds the chickens, while I have a good time. Good neighbour, it's a laugh when the chickens cluck: Little coquette, cock-a-doo, isn't that right? My husband is lovely and good, neighbour."

Pierre Passereau (fl. 1509 - 1547)

11. THE THREE RAVENS

Trad., arr. Thomas Ravenscroft
(c. 1582 - c. 1635)

1. The original text is spread over ten stanzas, because the first line is repeated three times.
2. Original reads "hey".

"Where shall we our break-fast take?"
well they can their ma-ster keep, with a down, der-ry, der-ry, der-ry, down, down.
great with young as she might go,

_____] with a down, hey der-ry, der-ry, down, down, down.

_____] with a down, der-ry, der-ry, down, down, down.

_____] with a down, down, der-ry, down, down.

3. Original "a"

Verse 4

Soprano
(others voices as before)

She lift___ up his blood-y head, down-a down, hey down, hey down, And
kissed his wounds that were so red, with a down. She got him up u-pon her back, And
car-ried him to an earth-en lake, with a down, der-ry, der-ry, der-ry, down, down.

Verse 5

Soprano
(others voices as before)

She bur-ried him be-fore the prime, down-a down, hey down, hey down, She was
dead her-self ere e'en-song time, with a down, God send___ e-v'ry gent-le-man Such
hawks, such hounds and such a le-man, with a down, der-ry, der-ry, der-ry, down, down.

12. THE APE, THE MONKEY AND BABOON

Thomas Weelkes (1576 – 1623)

their three na - tures was a sym - pa - thy. Nay,
bet - ter tricks in great men's hous - es lie. Tush,

na - tures was a sym - pa - thy. Nay,
tricks in great men's hous - es lie. Tush,

was a sym - pa - thy. Nay,
great men's hous - es lie. Tush,

mp repeat mf

quoth ba - boon, I do de - ny that strain: I
quoth ba - boon, when men do know I come, For

quoth ba - boon, I do de - ny that strain: I
quoth ba - boon, when men do know I come, For

quoth ba - boon, I do de - ny that strain: I
quoth ba - boon, when men do know I come, For

mf repeat f

have more knave - ry in me than you twain. twain.
sport from ci - ty, coun - try, they will run. run.

have more knave - ry in me than you twain. twain.
sport from ci - ty, coun - try, they will run. run.

have more knave - ry in me than you twain. twain.
sport from ci - ty, coun - try, they will run. run.

42

13. ROUNDS FROM THOMAS RAVENSCROFT'S "PAMMELIA" (1609)

(i) NEW OYSTERS

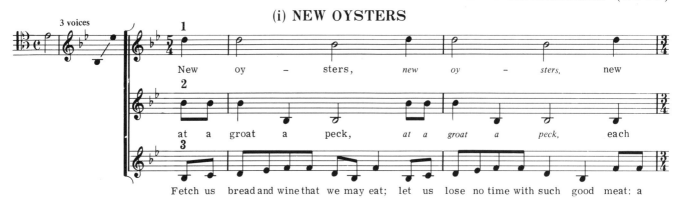

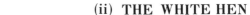

(ii) THE WHITE HEN

(iii) THE OLD DOG

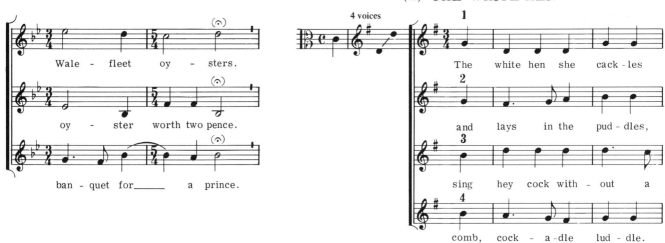

*Rest omitted in the original.

(iv) AS I ME WALKED

(v) LADY, COME DOWN AND SEE

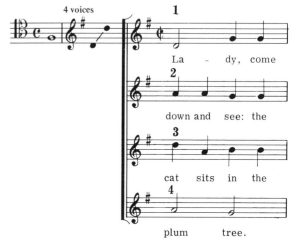

14. SEVENTEENTH CENTURY ROUNDS

(i) WELL RUNG TOM

Anon

(ii) MY DAME HATH A LAME TAME CRANE

Matthew White (fl. 1600-1630)

(iii) A CATCH ON THE MIDNIGHT CATS

Michael Wise (c. 1648–87)

EDITOR'S NOTES

I. General. This series is a thematic anthology of secular European madrigals and part-songs from the 16th and early 17th centuries. The settings are mainly for mixed four-part choir, but there are also some for three and five voices, and an occasional one for six. Five voices are strongly represented because this was an especially popular number in late 16th century madrigals. By and large, the items present relatively few vocal or harmonic difficulties for the fairly able choir, and where more than four parts are required, they are usually drawn from the upper voices (mainly the sopranos), with the tenor line hardly ever being split.

The term madrigal has been interpreted rather loosely. Besides the contrapuntal part-song, it relates to the frottola, ayre, chanson, lied and the villancico, whether courtly or folk (these all basically being harmonised melodies, often very simply set and usually repeated for each stanza). More obviously, it encompasses the ballet (a short stanzaic setting with repeats and fa la las), and the canzonet (a lighter style madrigal normally for a small number of voices). Rounds and catches have also been included because they were obviously an important component of a sing-song or a drinking party, certainly in 17th century England, and their choice of subject matter is very free-ranging. To help make madrigal concerts rather more of a party than a performance at least two or three of the rounds in each volume have been selected as simple enough to be sung by an audience with or without a visual aid (see section V, no.5 of these notes).

One of the most important features of this anthology is the arrangement by subjects, each volume being devoted to one of the prevalent topics in secular songs, for example, "The Animal Kingdom" (vol. 1), "Love and Marriage" (vol. 2) and "Desirable Women" (vol. 3). This provides not only a new approach to madrigal anthologies but also, more importantly, a focus for the singers and, it is hoped, a comprehensible, appetising programme for the audience. Thus, it should be possible to provide a short concert entirely from one of these volumes, and two halves of a longer concert from any two.

Each volume contains at least twelve part-songs and, on average, half a dozen rounds. About one-third of the texts are in English, but an attempt has been made to provide a representative collection of Italian and French lyrics, and, to a lesser extent, of German and Spanish. The selection combines indispensable popular works with a fair mixture of relatively unfamiliar but attractive and singable pieces. Some thought has also been given to affording a balance between the lively and the reflective, the happy and the sad, for the sake of variety of mood and to help mirror the ups and downs, real or imagined, of Renaissance life and love.

II. Editorial method. As with the Chester Latin Motet series, the Editor has endeavoured to make the volumes suitable for both performance and study. The madrigals are transposed, where necessary, into the most practical keys for ease of vocal range, are barred, fully underlaid in modernised spelling and punctuation, are provided with breathing marks, and have a simplified reduction as a rehearsal aid or as a basis for a continuo. Editorial tempi and dynamics have been supplied, but only in the reduction, leaving conductors free to supply their own according to their interpretation, vocal resources and the acoustics. The vocal range is given at the beginning of each piece, as also are translations for the non-English texts.

To help musicologists, the madrigals are transcribed from the most authoritative sources available. Original clefs, signatures and note values are given at the beginning and wherever they change during the course of a piece. Ligatures are indicated by slurs, editorial accidentals are placed above the stave, and the underlay is shown in italics when it expands a ditto sign, or in square brackets when it is entirely editorial. Where the original contains a *basso continuo* it is included as the bass line of the reduction. Instrumental parts (which appear only occasionally in these volumes, e.g., Ravenscroft's *Three Ravens*, item no. 11) are transcribed within the relevant vocal lines as well as in the reduction. Editorial emendations and alterations are given in footnotes within the text proper. Finally, each volume contains brief notes on the scope of the edition, the composers, stylistic features of the part-songs, and the sources used.

III. The themes and the lyrics. Anyone with even a cursory acquaintance with madrigals will be aware of the frequency of references to beasts, birds and insects in them. Many Renaissance writers, especially those from the Elizabethan period, saw in the animal kingdom a valuable source of commentary on the nature and state of mankind. They had inherited from classical and mediaeval authors a vast menagerie of real and fictitious creatures, and often consumed their legacy with astounding prodigality. Edmund Spenser constructed elaborate beast allegories on the contemporary situation at court, and Shakespeare, whose plays contain over four thousand beast references, found animal imagery an effective method of character portrayal.

Madrigal lyrics encompass a wide variety of creatures and employ them in several ways. To begin with there is the direct physical description of an animal *per se*, even to the point of imitating its sounds. The most obvious example is that of Banchieri's *Contrapunto Bestiale* (no. 2) where the cuckoo, owl, cat and dog vie with one another in counterpoint supported by a (drunken?) bass, possibly in some implied ironic commentary on the bestial nature of man deprived of reason. Another example is Lemlin's *Der Gutzgauch* (no. 7), with its banal folk lyrics sung against a duet of soprano cuckoos. Sometimes the total physical description is a parody or satire, as in the case of *El Grillo* (no. 4), though it is uncertain whether the cricket mimics a pompous Milanese singer named Grillo, or is a subtle hint to a patron that even the most dedicated musician requires adequate remuneration (cf. H. Osthoff, *Josquin Desprez*, 1965, II, p. 205).

The animals can also have a dramatic or narrative function. In *Il est Bel et Bon* (no. 10), the pecking chickens taunt both the hoodwinked husband and the flighty wife by appearing to cackle: "Co-co-coquette", and by superb mastery the composer makes the dialogue of the two women assume the sound of a hen-party. The interrelationship of creatures and humans is also vividly portrayed. *Une Puce* (no. 8), an early song in a very rich tradition of sung flea execrations, depicts both the hopping movements of the insect and the tormented scratchings of its blood-donor; while *Audite Nova* (no. 5) celebrates the cooking and eating of St Martin's especially favoured bird, the goose, during the German festival on the saint's day, 11th November.

In the more reflective lyrics (whether in seriousness or jest), the description of the animal is the starting-point of the meditation from which the poet then draws, by analogy, his general or personal message and conclusion. In the first of the two swan songs in this volume, *Il Bianco e Dolce Cigno* (no. 1), the lover contrasts and parallels his approach to death, both actual and sexual, with the swan's, pointing the paradox that while the swan, though singing, dies disconsolate, he, though weeping, would happily die a thousand deaths of love and desire. Several authors have been proposed for this lovely Petrarchan lyric, though the likeliest, according to Alfred Einstein (*The Italian Madrigal,* vol. 1, 1949, p.186), is Alfonso d' Avolos. The second piece, The *Silver Swan* (no. 3) begins with the same notion of the death of the swan, but expands the description (e.g., "Leaning her breast against the reedy shore . . .") and delays the message to the final couplet, which contains the general observation that just as more geese than swans survive, so do more fools than wise men. If, as seems possible, the verse is by Sir Walter Ralegh, who spent many years languishing in the Tower, then the comment relates to James I's court and to Ralegh's predicament. This interpretation is especially ironic because Ralegh himself seems to have been nicknamed "goose" from time to time (see article cited below). In the mock-serious *Petite Importune Mouche* (no. 6) there is a further comparison between the creature and the individual, yet another frustrated lover, who enviously imagines the lucky fly buzzing over the loved one, enjoying an uninterrupted view of her beauty and even sampling it at very close quarters.

As might be expected, the nightingale also frequently features in the reflective madrigal, since in every age its song seems to have captivated the soul of the tortured romantic. In the exquisite lyric by Guarini, *Dolcissimo Usignolo* (no. 9), the lover, like the one in the fly madrigal, though less grudgingly, descants on the happiness of the innocent nightingale and his own unhappy wingless fate, much as Burns was to in his own sublime expression of a similar pathetic fallacy, *Ye Banks and Braes.*

Several traditional literary devices are present in these animal lyrics, most notably, prosopopoeia, whereby the creatures talk and actually debate as humans (cf. Chaucer's *Parliament of Birds* and Skelton's *Speak Parrot*). The technique is employed in various genres, for example, the ballad, as in *The Three Ravens* (no. 11) or a form of Aesopian fable, as with *The Ape, the Monkey and Baboon* (no. 12). In *The Three Ravens,* the birds are only the starting-point of the story. They are the predators looking for their next meal of carrion, thwarted by the immolatory doe who buries the slain knight — a strange symbolic tale which may have connections with the *Corpus Christi Carol.* The trio in no. 12, by contrast, are not part of a ritualistic ballad, but creatures of social satire in the tradition of Aristophanes as well as Aesop, since they literally ape the manners of men. If, as is at least remotely possible, actual individuals are hinted at, then the satire may well be personal and political too. (See further, the article cited below, which demonstrates that Sir Robert Cecil, later Earl of Salisbury, was known as "The Ape"). Actual political songs have been excluded from this collection, though several exist, including Dowland's "It was a time when silly bees could speak", which is a setting of a lyric ascribed to the Earl of Essex.

Rounds are, on the whole, far less subtle in their treatment of animals, usually being content with depicting elementary sounds such as the twitter of birds and the barking of dogs, or perpetrating simple bawdy puns with obvious reference to cuckoldry. Sophistication does evolve in the 17th century, however, as in the case of the round, *Ye Cats that at Midnight* (no. 14 iii), which is a very clever mixture of Petrarchan parody with what was later to be called a bawdy barrack-room ballad.

The poets of animals are not, on the whole, astute students of natural history, and many of their notions are borrowed, uncritically or for literary convenience, from the classical naturalists such as Pliny. Thus, they continue with the notion that the swan sang only when it was about to die (nos. 1 and 3), that the cricket was a bird (no. 4) and that, as in the Dowland *Silly Bees* song, the queen bee was a king bee. For further reading see Beryl Rowland, *Animals with Human Faces,* London, 1974, and Anthony G. Petti, "Beasts and Politics in Elizabethan Literature", *Essays and Studies,* London, 1963, pp. 68-90. The twenty animals in this volume are listed here alphabetically, the page numbers being in parenthesis when the references are fleeting.

		Page				Page
1.	Ape	40		11.	Fly	19
2.	Baboon	40		12.	Goose (Geese)	(11), 15
3.	Cat(s), Kittens	5, 42 v, 43 i, iii		13.	Hawks	(38)
4.	Chickens, Hen	34, 42 ii		14.	Horse	(40)
5.	Crane	43 ii		15.	Monkey	40
6.	Cricket	12		16.	Nightingale	27
7.	Cuckoo	5, 22, 42 iv, 43 i		17.	Owl	5
8.	Doe	38		18.	Oysters	42 i
9.	Dog	5, 42 iii		19.	Ravens	38
10.	Flea	24		20.	Swan(s)	2, 9

IV. The Music. In the best madrigals of the later Renaissance, words and music are successfully married, the music being descriptive of the intellectual and emotive meaning of the lyric. Reflecting the nuances of the words is obviously easier in a through-composed madrigal than in the stanzaic ayre or chanson, but even in these the setting often provides the highest common factor for the content of the different stanzas, as in Dowland (e.g. *Come Again,* vol. 2) and Le Jeune (e.g. *Une Puce,* no. 8). Word-painting is a common mode of musical description, especially in the animal madrigals, as the present selection amply demonstrates.

This series fittingly begins with a madrigal by "the most excellent and divine" Arcadelt (c. 1505-68), since he was one of the greatest of the earlier madrigalists. Concerning his nationality and life much conjecture abounds. Though usually supposed to be Flemish, he may well have been French, in which case his Christian name should be Jacques and not Jacob. Further, it is surmised that in his earlier years he came under the influence of Philippe Verdelot, and that he spent some time in Florence (post 1532) and Venice (c. 1539). From 1540 he was in Papal service, when he became acquainted with Michelangelo. He went to France in 1551, and from 1554-62 was in the service of Charles of Lorraine, later Archbishop of Rheims. He also seems to have served the king of France for a short period.

Arcadelt's secular works form the bulk of his output, comprising over one hundred chansons and two hundred madrigals, and he excelled in both forms. The chansons are generally full of vitality and rhythmic energy (e.g. *Margot Labourez les Vignes,* in volume 3) and the madrigals are graceful, compact, translucent and of exquisite melodic beauty as evidenced by the present example, *Il Bianco e Dolce Cigno,* possibly the most popular Italian madrigal ever written. It is an early work, being published in *Il Primo Libro di Madrigali d'Archadelt,* Venice, Antonio Gardano (first extant edition, 1539, transcribed here from the set of copies in the Bayerische Staatsbibliothek, Munich). The whole collection was so successful that it was reprinted at least forty-three times. *Il Bianco e Dolce Cigno* has the serenity and poignancy of a restrained Lenten motet in the style of Palestrina, the music delicately pointing and controlling the sadness of the text, while suggesting in its gently undulating phrases the graceful gliding of the swan. The setting is mainly homophonic. Lightness of touch for the opening is helped by delaying the entry of the bass, and then a slight acerbity is added by the sudden F natural chord for "piangendo" (bars 6 and 11). The final section fans out into a little expressive fugue with a leaping opening figure and climactic sequence to depict the bitter-sweet desire for a lover's death.

Adriano Banchieri (1568-1634), apart from being a talented composer with great comic invention, was one of the most distinguished organists of his generation, and, soon after becoming a Benedictine monk in 1590, he moved from monastery to monastery as visiting organist, sometimes actually inaugurating an organ. However, his main position was at San Michele in Bosco, near Bologna where he was born and died. Though he wrote a large amount of sacred music, very little of which is performed today, his secular music is also extremely copious, considering that he was a monk. Most of the madrigals he composed are linked thematically in the form of masking comedy, sometimes in the style of the *comoedia dell'arte* and featuring its stock characters. Somewhat in this vein is his well-known five-part collection entitled *Festino nella Sera del Giovedi Grasso avanti Cena,* 1608 (Night festival for before supper on Fat Thursday). Such a piece would have been performed on the last Thursday of the pre-Lent carnival. Since Rome and Venice were the chief centres for the carnival, it was appropriate that the *Festino* should be published in Venice. (A complete set of copies is housed, amongst other places, in the Bibliothèque Royale, Brussels, from which the *Contrapunto Bestiale* is transcribed here.) Banchieri obviously considered the *Contrapunto* a show-piece, for it is announced at length in the preceding madrigal, *Capriciata a tre voci.* As in all the Banchieri pieces in the collection, a reader is supposed to tell the audience what they are going to hear — in this case: "Un cane, un cucco, un gatto, un chiu per spasso,/Far contrapunto a mente sopra un basso." (A dog, cuckoo, cat and a screech-owl make counterpoint on a bass). The phonetically represented animal sounds, enclosed by fa la las (a b a), are a good guide to the Italian accents of these Renaissance creatures, whose counterpoint is sometimes halting (the cuckoos falter towards the end). An inebriated basso provides a continuo with lyrics hardly more illuminating than the noises his line is supposed to prop up.

In contrast to the *Contrapunto* is an almost equally celebrated piece, the second of the swan songs, by another eminent organist and composer, Orlando Gibbons (1583-1625). Though born in Oxford, Gibbons became a chorister of King's College Cambridge under his brother Edward (1596-8), and took a B.Mus. from Cambridge in 1606, capping it with a D.Mus. in 1622. He was soon held in high favour at court and became senior organist of the Chapel Royal. He also had the distinction of being organist at Westminster Abbey. Though his output in sacred music is sizeable, Gibbons published only one book of madrigals, and even these are on solemn or sad texts: *The First Set of Madrigals and Mottets, apt for Viols and Voyces,* London, 1612. The practice of making the lower parts optional for voices or instruments (or mixed) tends to concentrate attention on top voice, and this is certainly true of *The Silver Swan,* the first item in the collection (transcribed here from the British Library part-books). Nevertheless, the madrigal is well integrated, and all the parts save the middle one have very melodious lines, even if they are somewhat instrumental. Some of the ideas seem to derive from the Arcadelt setting: the smooth undulating beginning, and the quasi-fugal treatment of the final section; but whereas in the Arcadelt there is a leaping figure followed by a gentle descent, in the Gibbons the soprano has a bold series of sequential dropping fifths, thus emphasising the dying fall of the text.

The next composer, Josquin des Près (c.1440-1521), by common agreement in his time and now, is considered one of the greatest and most versatile composers of the Renaissance, as well as one of the most prolific. His long and varied life is almost as conjectural as Arcadelt's, even concerning his birthplace and nationality, opinion swinging towards his being considered French rather than Flemish. Josquin's early years seem to have been spent in Milan, as a singer, first at Milan Cathedral (1459-72) and then for the Sforzas, particularly Cardinal Ascanio Sforza (1479-86). He went to Rome with this patron, working partly in the Cardinal's chapel and partly in the Papal chapel. Towards the end of the century Josquin left for France, where he probably became attached to the court of Louis XII. He returned to Italy for a brief spell in Ferrara, and then went back to France and the Low Countries, dying in Condé.

For those who know Josquin through the long and often solemn, devotional motets and masses, his handful of *frottole* such as *Scaramella* and *El Grillo,* with their light-hearted texts and sense of humour in transparently simple settings, must come as a shock. *El Grillo* was first published by the famous early anthologist of *frottole,* Petrucci, in *Frottole Libro Tertio* (transcribed from copy in Bayerische Staatsbibliothek, Munich). Unpretentious and homophonic, it has, despite separate sections, a continuity of movement akin to perpetual motion. The sound of the cricket is conveyed in diverse ways: for example, in the rising dotted canon of the alto and tenor (bars 7-10) against the long note of the soprano, and more especially in the antiphonal patter of "Dalle beve" (11-16). The rhythm constantly shifts, and develops into a type of Spanish dance in the final section (28-37). Whichever and whatever the satire in the piece (which seems more likely to be mimicry of a Milanese singer with Spanish pretentions rather than a hint to a not normally niggardly Cardinal Sforza — see Section IV) the piece can stand on its own in sense of fun and *joie de vivre.*

Orlandus Lassus or Orlande de Lassus (1532-94) is the Josquin of his period: brilliant, versatile and prolific. In his youth he travelled widely in the service of Fernando Gonzaga, a general of Charles V, though based in the Low Countries. Having gone with Gonzaga to Italy, he continued his travels there under several patrons. In 1563 he obtained the important post of *maestro di cappella* at St. John Lateran, but soon left to renew his travels. He joined the court of Albrecht V in Munich and became his *Kapellmeister* in 1563, holding the post until his death, despite frequent absences.

The Lassus canon encompasses every type of sacred and secular choral music. His German lieder form a substantial collection, being mainly extrovert drinking or love songs with a tinge of satire. They are couched in a lively, declamatory style, as exemplified by *Audite Nova* (*Sechs Deutsche Lieder,* Munich, Adam Berg, 1573, transcribed from copies in Österreichische Nationalbibliothek, Musiksammlung). It begins in the style of a Latin motet celebrating Christmas. Then, bathetically, it moves into swift homophonic narrative about a farmer's goose and its nice long neck. Next, moving into an awkward triple time it conveys the impression of a hungry salivating mob in the climatic imperatives of cooking and eating the bird, before returning to duple time and further imperatives for wine to accompany the food. (Interestingly enough, the final section of this madrigal (60-65) contains a passage of syncopated writing very similar to the ending of *Non Habemus Regem* in William Byrd's *Crowd Responses* to the *Matthew Passion.)*

The next composer, Claude Le Jeune (c. 1530-1600), lived a charmed life, being a Huguenot in 16th century France. Fortunately, he was patronised by Henry of Navarre, and became household composer to him when he acceded as Henry IV. Though born in Valenciennes, Le Jeune lived mainly in Paris and died there. Most of his composing was directed towards vernacular setting of the psalms, of which nearly three hundred and fifty survive, but he also wrote over one hundred secular pieces, sixty-six being chansons. These are in light-hearted Parisian style and follow his own theories of clear settings which observe the contours and rhythm of the words in mainly homophonic style. The two chansons included here, *Petite Importune Mouche* and *Une Puce* are both transcribed from the 1608 edition of *Airs,* being nos. 17 and 20 respectively (complete set in Bibliothèque Sainte Geneviève). The fly chanson has a delicate, almost filigree melody and a remarkably flexible rhythm. Melismas are occasionally used to smooth the progressions, though rarely in the top line. A mock-heroic yearning is preserved throughout, being intensified in the alternative five-part conclusion. By contrast, the flea chanson is all jerkiness and frenzy, indicated by the swift and constantly changing rhythms and note values. The hopping of the insect, the itching of the victim, the pain, the frustration and the call for help are all admirably conveyed by the music of this splendid vignette.

Lorenz Lemlin (c. 1496-1549) is a comparatively lightweight German composer, though he was an effective and influential teacher. He graduated from Heidelberg in 1514, became a priest and was appointed Kappellmeister to Ludwig V, whose court was at Heidelberg. Among his pupils was Georg Forster, who is best known for publishing an anthology of German lieder, including those of this fellow pupils and his teacher. The small amount of Lemlin's work that has survived includes a handful of motets and fifteen secular songs, of which the best known is *Der Gutzgauch.* This was published in the Forster collection (*Frische Teutsche Liedlein,* 1539-56, now available in a modern edition), but has been transcribed here from the manuscript in the Deutsche Staatsbibliothek, Berlin (MS. P.W. 94). Using the sound of the cuckoo in song is a very old tradition which probably predates even *Sumer is icumen in.* But whereas the old six-part round uses the two cuckoos in the burden, Lemlin employs them as descants in the sopranos. The piece is lively, accomplished, and mercifully brief, and despite the sophistication of six parts is very much in a folk song tradition.

Yet another of the giants of Renaissance and Early Baroque music is represented in this volume in the person of Claudio Monteverdi (1567-1643). He was something of a child prodigy, publishing his first collection of sacred music when he was sixteen, and his second a year later. After being tutored by Marc'Antonio Ingenieri in his native Cremona, he entered the service of the magnificent Gonzaga court at Mantua in 1589, becoming director of music in 1601. He left Mantua for Venice in 1612 and a year later was appointed to the highly coveted post of *maestro di cappella* at St Mark's in 1613, retaining it until his death. Monteverdi excelled in all forms of composition, including masses, motets, the famous Vespers, operas and innumerable books of madrigals. His *Dolcissimo Usignolo* is a late work, being published in his *Madrigali Guerrieri et Amorosi, con Alcuni Opusculi,* Venice, 1638 (transcribed from the copies in the Liceo Musicale, Bologna). With one other in the collection, *Vago Augelletto,* it is in *stilo franchese,* which apparently signifies the employment of metrical patterns for the text and perhaps, too, a chanson style, with a clean break for sections. The first soprano intones, much as it does in *Beatus Vir,* against a simple continuo (here reconstructed from the choral repeat). This device, coupled with the high tessitura of the top line, clearly points to high, delicate warbles of the "most sweet nightingale". The total effect of the madrigal is of sublime and wistful mellifluousness. The utterance is also fairly personal and intimate, especially in the use of solos, close third duets, trios and quartets, the bass being reserved for reinforcement and final repetitions.

For centuries the next composer, Pierre Passereau (fl. 1509-47), lacked not only a biography but even a Christian name. It is now known that he sang tenor in the chapel of the Duke of Angoulême (later Francis I) and at Bourges Cathedral. Very little of his music survives — twenty-three chansons and one motet (published in volume 8 of the *Chester Latin Motet* series) — yet he was sufficiently popular to be anthologised by Attaignant, and his lively, impish and slightly obscene chansons earned him a place among the "merry musicians" mentioned by Rabelais. *Il est Bel et Bon,* a *tour de force* and deservedly his best known piece, was first published by Attaignant in 1534. It is transcribed here from the corrected edition of 1536, *Tiers Livre Contentant XXI Chansons Musicales,* Paris (complete set in the Bibliothèque Mazarine, Paris). The handling of the dialogue of the two women is masterly in this fast flowing, frothy madrigal. Throughout there is a sense of clucking and pecking from the two women as well as from the chickens. Occasionally the crowing gets louder, as in the fifth rise on "commère" (35ff.) and in the exciting cackling counterpoint of "co-co-dae" against "petite coquette" (43ff.). The return to the opening refrain gives the work a circular effect of amusing futility.

As with Passereau, some progress has been made in recent years on the biography of Thomas Ravenscroft. There is now, for example, an approximation of his life-span: c. 1582-1635. It is thought that he was a chorister of Chichester cathedral and then of St. Paul's, and that he obtained his B.Mus. from Cambridge c.1605. Though it is clear that he was responsible for composing the *Whole Booke of Psalmes* (1621) and the examples in his music treatise, it is unclear what precisely he composed in his three books of songs, rounds and catches: *Pammelia* and *Deuteromelia* (1609), and *Melismata* (1611). It is likely that his main function was as editor, though even this is an impressive achievement, since his are the first collections of published rounds, which number over a hundred. In the case of *The Three Ravens* (*Melismata,* edited from British Library copy), Ravenscroft seems to have taken the already popular melody and added an accompaniment for optional voices or instruments. As with all his arrangements, the accompaniment is simple and effective, and the style fully accords with the melody and text of the ballad.

The madrigal section of this volume concludes with a short piece by a near-contemporary of Ravenscroft, Thomas Weelkes (c. 1576- 1623). Yet another composer-organist, Weelkes was a man of great talents who seems to have gone to seed through drunkenness. He was appointed organist of Winchester College in 1598, and then c. 1601 became organist and choral instructor at Chichester. In 1602 he obtained a B.Mus. from New College Oxford, and by 1608 was a Gentleman Extraordinary of the Chapel Royal, though he was dismissed for being drunk and disorderly in 1617. Weelkes's earlier madrigal collections are very rich and sophisticated (as, for example, in the double-madrigal, *Thule, the Period of Cosmography*). His last collection, from which the present work is taken, is very modest: *Ayres or Phantasticke Spirites for Three Voices,* London, 1608 (copy in British Library). As the title of the collection implies, the texts are rather zany, and the melody is in the top line. The settings are tuneful but unadventurous, being short and mainly homophonic. Though it is not as lively as *Come, Sirrah Jack, Ho,* the most famous item in the collection, *The Ape, the Monkey and Baboon* is suitably whimsical and pleasant, and the text is a useful piece of social satire (see section III).

The rounds by Ravenscroft are typical of the material in his three main collections. They are brief, interesting, easy to sing, and based on lively, everyday subjects. The first two rounds of item no. 14 are very much in the Ravenscroft tradition. *Well Rung, Tom* is anonymous, though Mary C. Taylor (*Rounds on Rounds,* p. 59) lists it as by J. Miller. It is transcribed here from the fourth and enlarged edition of Playford's *Second Book of the Pleasant Musical Companion* (1701), copy in the British Library. *My Dame hath a Lame Tame Crane* (published in Hilton's *Catch that Catch Can,* 1667 edition, copy in the British Library) is by Matthew White, a minister and a bass singer from Wells who became a member of the Chapel Royal and took a B.Mus. from Oxford in 1629. This round is delightful nonsense to sing, and, like most of the rounds in this anthology, is within an easily manageable vocal range.

The last of the rounds is by the intriguing singer and composer, Michael Wise (c. 1648-87). Like Weelkes, he made an auspicious start and was a Gentleman of the Chapel Royal by 1676; but he was knocked on the head, quite literally, by the Salisbury Watch for his unruliness, and died from the blow. His round, *Ye Cats that at Midnight* (transcribed from Playford's *Second Book of the Pleasant Musical Companion,* 1685, copy in the British Library), is the most sophisticated of the examples published here, both in music and lyrics, and is somewhat in the style of Purcell. Though a little plodding and with a duller middle line than Purcell would have allowed, the total effect is of a majestic mock heroic invocation, a description which typifies many of the more ebullient madrigals in this collection.

V. Notes on Programming. The performance of a concert according to themes can be augmented and enhanced in a number of ways. The following points are suggested by the Editor in the light of his experience in directing concerts for a general audience:

1. Include some solo items on the same theme, for example, John Bartlet's *Of all the Birds that I Do Know,* Dowland's *It was a Time when Silly Bees,* and two or three of Ravenscroft's songs with chorus, e.g., *It was a Frog in the Well* and *Tomorrow the Fox will come to Town.* Ideas can be gleaned for English songs as well as madrigals by looking through the revised E. H. Fellowes, *English Madrigal Verse* (1967). There are also several useful instrumental pieces, for example, many of those set or arranged by Morley: *Il Grillo, La Rondinella* (the house-martin), *La Tortorella* (the little dove) and the famous *Frog Galliard,* originally set by John Dowland.

2. Briefly introduce each item or group of items much as Banchieri suggests for his *Contrapunto Bestiale* (see section IV above), and highlight one or two of the salient stylistic features. For foreign madrigals it is useful to read a translation even if one is provided in the programme.

3. A concert can be filled out and given variety by introducing occasional readings from drama, poetry or prose of the period, either to supplement or contrast with the madrigals. For example, the passage concerning Launce and his dog from Shakespeare's *Two Gentlemen of Verona* (Act II, scene 3) is very effective, especially with a live dog; and John Donne's *The Flea* is a good companion piece to Le Jeune's *Une Puce.* Numerous anthologies of Renaissance verse and prose are available to assist the search for material, including the *Oxford Book of 16th Century Verse* (containing such items as Philip Sidney's poem on the nightingale, p.182, and Spenser's sonnet, "The Merry Cuckoo") and the *Oxford Book of 17th Century Verse.* Similar anthologies are put out by Penguin Books, who also publish a *Penguin Book of Bird Poetry,* which can be supplemented by Samuel Carr's *The Poetry of Birds.* Useful prose passages can be gleaned from Edward Topsell's *Historie of Foure-Footed Beasts,* 1607, recently reprinted, which also has lots of illustrations. A general book for gleaning ideas is Emma Phipson's *Animal-Lore of Shakespeare's Time,* first published in 1883 and reprinted in 1976. The Beryl Rowland book cited in section 3 has a helpful bibliography.

4. If conditions allow, a cyclorama or screen can be employed for a backdrop of slides of animals from works of art roughly contemporaneous with the pieces performed. Thus, for the flea items something equivalent to George Latour's *Servant with a Flea* could be shown (provided there are no copyright difficulties). For the Weelkes piece on the monkey, ape and baboon, the Younger Teniers *Monkies at an Inn* would be suitable. Ideas for illustrations can be readily obtained from the innumerable art books on the Renaissance, among them Bernard Berenson's *The Italian Painters of the Renaissance* (1952, etc.) the very first plate of which illustrates a Crivelli peacock. The various art books